# GETTIN' LUCKY WITH THE PACK

OMEGAVERSE HOLIDAY QUICKIES

CLOVER HOLLOWAY

Book Cover: Unfortunate Designs

Independently Published by Unfortunate Productions LLC

Print ISBN: 979-8-9913742-9-3

# BLURB

Brianna and her alpha are having a quick tryst behind the bar they work at, McGinty's, when one of their regulars catches them in the act. Except, not only has she had a crush on this patron for quite a while, he's also her scent match. Will they get luck and bring a third into their little pack this holiday?

*Omegaverse Holiday Quickies are novelettes with more smut than plot. They are meant to be a fun escape with no angst that you can read in one sitting. Have fun and get your spice on!*

*To everyone who's ever had to work at an Irish themed bar on St. Patrick's Day. I've been there.*

# AUTHOR'S NOTE

A note about the Omegaverse Holiday Quickies series. We all love Omegaverse books with lots of character development and conflict resolution, and of course heats, but sometimes you just want a short little palate cleanser to read in between longer novels, or while you're in the waiting room at the doctor's office, or the school pick up line...you catch my drift.

That's where the Omegaverse Holiday Quickies series comes in! I love reading those short instalove/instalust where a OTT man falls hard and fast for a damsel he rescued from the woods/mountain/mafia/ex/etc, but I usually only find them in the contemporary genres. I wanted to capture that same vibe but with an Omegaverse twist.

All of these stories will be of existing packs, or insta-love pack formation, with no angst or third act breakups. They are very short, and meant to be fast, fun, and totally smutty.

They are also light on the Omegaverse pitfalls, and won't always center around a heat. The spice will be spicin' though, I promise you that! If you aren't familiar with Omegaverse, take a look at the short primer I included next.

All my books are queer. The worlds they are set in are queer-normative and there will always be a wide mix of relationship pairings, dynamics, and genders. Even if the primary relationship is a man and a woman, all my characters are pan unless otherwise stated. If that's not something you're comfortable with, my books likely aren't for you.

There are also explicit adult scenes mixed with a healthy dose of kink. Please read the content considerations before diving in.

I really hope you love this series, because I have so many ideas for more holiday quickies!

Stay lucky,
Clover

# WHAT IS OMEGAVERSE?

Omegaverse is a subgenre that takes place in an alternate universe loosely based on canid culture. Similar to wolf shifters, they form packs and have a hierarchy, but there are no shifters in my Omegaverse. There are different *designations* of people - most commonly alpha, beta, and omega. Each Omegaverse may have different designations, rules, and lore depending on the author. In this primer the rules will be specific to the universe I created for these characters, and some details may not be the same as you've read before.

Some things most every Omegaverse has in common though are designations (A/B/O), heats, scents, and knots.

**Alphas**

Alphas are usually the strongest and most dominant members of society. They are usually big and muscular, and some may have more *alpha power* than others. They can *bark* other designations into submission, forcing them to follow their commands. They also have a special feature at the base of their penises called a *knot*. The knot will swell when the alpha orgasms, and if they are having penetrative sex then it will *lock* them inside their partner. Alphas can be driven into a *rut* when overly aroused.

Alphas are often in positions of power and will behave based on their alpha instincts. Their scents are strong and they will bite a partner to *bond* them.

## Betas

Betas are what most people would consider a "regular" person. They are the most common designation in society and aren't as affected by hormones and pheromones. They do not have knots and won't go into a rut.

There are some worlds where betas may be considered less valuable because they are essentially normal humans. In this world, betas are known to be excellent additions to packs because they are level-headed and can balance out the extremes of alphas and omegas.

## Omegas

Omegas are usually the rarest and most valued designation in society. Because of their low numbers, one omega may form a pack with several alphas and betas. Omegas are generally submissive and natural caretakers. Omegas have heats where their bodies drive them to breed. They will have insatiable sexual appetites and they may need several partners to satisfy them. If omegas are not knotted during their heat, it can be extremely painful and sometimes dangerous for the omega.

In some worlds, omegas may be considered the lowest rung of society, and even like property. They could be barred from getting jobs or may be otherwise controlled by their families or their alphas. They can be any gender and sometimes assigned male at birth (AMAB) people can get pregnant.

## Heats and Ruts

This is a state where omegas and alphas are completely driven by their hormones to copulate. The heat could be on a regular schedule much like a woman's period, or they could be unpredictable. Both options are common tropes in the genre. When in a heat or rut, omegas will often beg for a *bonding bite*, and alphas are driven to *bite* and *claim* their omegas.

These episodes may be controlled by *heat suppressants* or *rut blockers*.

## Scent Matches

Scent is super important in Omegaverse. Everyone has some type of scent, everything from sandalwood to strawberry shortcake and more. Alphas and omegas will have the strongest scents, and betas will have milder scents. When someone finds someone with a scent that is utterly irresistible, they are *scent matches*. This is akin to fated mates. Some universes will have different levels of scent matches (scent sympathetic, scent match, soul scent, etc).

Often if there is an incompatible alpha or omega, then they will smell terrible to the main characters. Usually their scents can indicate mood, souring or burning when they are upset, or sweeter when they are aroused. Mates will often *scent mark* each other by rubbing their *scent glands* or cheeks along the other's skin to *claim* each other.

## Mates/Bonding

As you read above, scent matches often indicate mates. When an alpha claims a beta or omega, they will bite them to mark them with a *bonding bite*. The bonds will work differently in each universe, but most commonly bonded mates will have a two way mental connection where they can sense each other's moods. Sometimes alphas will force bonds on people who are not their willing mates, and sometimes you have to accept the connection for a bond to stick. Sometimes only the alphas need to make the bite, but sometimes both partners need to claim each other to complete the bond. This is probably the most varied tenet in Omegaverse and it doesn't mean any one is incorrect.

# CONTENT CONSIDERATIONS

This is an adult story with explicit sexual content. It's more smut than plot. Like, way more. The characters in this story are pansexual may have different relationships with each other. That's my nice way of saying everyone is probably boinking everyone.

In addition to St. Patrick's Day shenanigans, you'll find MFM explicit scenes, mild SA (unwanted ass grabbing), threat of violence, alcohol and marijuana use (on page), fingering, oral sex, voyeurism, exhibitionism, semi-public sex, degradation, unprotected sex, cream pies, snowballing, biting, bonding, knotting, unsanitary banging environment, and a whole lot of green clothing.

# 1

"Behind!"

I automatically push my hips forward against the speed well at the warning, continuing to pour the seven shots of Jame-o the frat boys in front of me ordered. A hand grazes my hip as Truett passes behind me to make his way to the other end of the bar.

Even with the air full of competing scents from the patrons, his brandied pear scent manages to stand out and wrap around me. I learned early on to wear slick panties whenever I had a shift with the hot-as-sin alpha—which is nearly every shift I work, honestly. Does that make me lucky or unlucky? Jury's still out on that one.

Working at a sorta-kinda Irish bar on St. Patrick's day isn't for the weak. The main room of McGinty's is a sea of green-clad revelers whose only goal is to get drunk enough they start believing their brogue is passable. Spoiler alert: it's not.

Dropping the meager tip the frat boys left me into the bucket, I shift my attention to the next patron and immediately give him a genuine smile. Liam is a regular here, one I'm always happy to see.

"I didn't expect to see you today," I yell across the bartop.

He raises a brow and smirks as he leans in so he doesn't have to raise his voice to be heard over the crowd."And miss seeing my favorite girl in action?"

His words shouldn't give me butterflies, it's just simple flirting. Something we do every time he's in here. Yet, those damn winged assholes are currently fluttering up a storm in my stomach. Someone call pest control, I can't keep feeling this way every time his rich green eyes connect with mine.

Customers flirt with me all the time because, let's face it, I'm hot. I know what I look like, and I'm not about to downplay my looks when I work damn hard on my appearance. Usually I can play it off, it's only Liam's flirting that turns me into a bumbling teenager.

Crossing my arms, I raise a brow in his direction. Before I can volley back a cute one-liner, a disheveled man nearly crashes face-first into the bartop, his shoulder knocking Liam aside.

"Watch it, asshole," the guy slurs, glaring at Liam like it was his fault. Liam doesn't engage, so the idiot loses interest and looks me up and down before hollering his drink order, spittle flinging from his lips. Gross.

"Twooo... wait no, three car bombs. Four if you wanna join me and my pack and s-swallow down some cream." The guy snorts like he just made the funniest joke. Jesus fucking Christ. It's a good thing I make bank on this holiday every year or this pathetic excuse for an alpha would be getting his Guinness poured over his head instead of down his throat.

Wanting the man to go away, I hurriedly pour his three

half-pints of stout and shots of irish creme liquor. I don't know how he's going to carry all that back to his friends, but that's not my problem.

"Last name?" I ask pointedly.

"Uh, Fremont. Freeeeee-monnnt," he drags the name out like that will help me understand him better. I give him a curt nod and turn to the POS to ring in his drinks to his tab, thankful he's managed to stumble off somewhere by the time I'm done.

Liam's lips are rolled tight, like he's trying to hold in his laughter. "Does he know that ordering one of those in a real Irish pub would get his ass beat?"

The deadpan look I give him screams my answer without words, and he lets out a hearty laugh. Fuck, I want to hear him laugh like that more often.

"HEY!"

I whip my head in the direction of the shout just in time to see Truett vaulting over the bar, eyes locked onto one of the platforms our Lucky Charms dance on. Most people respect the promo girls enough not to mess with them, but every once in a while some idiot thinks the rules don't apply to them. We have bouncers, but Truett is closer.

Welp, looks like that guy's night is about to take a depressing turn.

# 2

Fuck, I hate men. Yeah, I am a man and I still stand by that statement. The male species as a whole is pretty trash in my opinion. I'd like to think I'm one of the good ones, but I'm not infallible.

I'm not a creep, though. Unlike the guy I'm currently dragging up the worn wooden stairs in preparation to toss out on his ass.

When he grabbed Marley's ass and pushed her into her beer tub, my alpha protective instincts took over and before I knew what I was doing, I had a hand on the bar and was flying over the top of it. Marley is a bonded omega, but that doesn't stop alphas and even betas from harassing her. She's worked here for a couple years now, and I will always take care of family—whether blood or found.

The big brute thrashes as he stumbles up the last few steps beside me. "What the fuck, man? You're kickin' me out because of some dumb bitch?"

Now just at the door, I stop and spin to face the jerk. His face is red and sweaty—whether from anger or alcohol, I'm not sure. The cauliflower ear tells me he's not a stranger to fighting, so as much as I'd like to deck him, he prolly wouldn't go down easy. Sighing, I drag him past the wide-eyed host, out to the sidewalk, pushing him toward Mike, the big alpha who's working the door tonight. He's also Marley's mate. Mike catches the blustering asshole on instinct, then raises a brow at me in question.

"He pushed Marls into her tub. By grabbing her ass." I state by way of explanation. Mike's eyes darken as he looks back at the now simpering man in his grip, but I head back inside. Let him handle it. I gotta get back to the bar anyway, I left Bri solo.

Trotting down the stairs, I have to hop side to side to avoid several drunk patrons and pass the deejay booth on my way to the main bar. But when I finally set my sights on who's tending, confusion and worry sets in. Instead of Bri's sexy smile and brown ponytail, Lana is in her place, Johnny working alongside her.

Slipping behind the bar, I catch Lana's eye and she knows what I'm going to ask.

"She's taking a break out back." She nods her head in the direction of the kitchen meaningfully. "We got this for a while."

Giving her a grateful wave, I head through the back dining room, straight through the hot-as-fuck kitchen, and out the back door that leads to the now-closed underground garage. Sure enough, her tantalizing scent of black currant and jasmine winds through my senses, and I'm suddenly filled with need.

Rounding the corner, my cock hardens further when I see Brianna leaning casually against a large concrete column. The picture of nonchalance unless you know her. In reality, she's drawn tight as a bow string, her breath hitching as she hears me approach her. I don't waste time. I walk straight up to her and grab her ponytail, digging my fingertips in the strands near her scalp and tugging her head back with a growl.

"Did you sneak out here knowing I'd need you, omega?" I ask against her lips. She whines, so I tug her hair tighter. "Well?"

"Mhmmm. Yes, alpha. It's so fucking hot when you go all protector mode." She jerks forward and nips my bottom lip, hard. "And you always need to fuck if you don't get to fight," she purrs.

Her hand dives between us to cup my cock through my khaki shorts, but I need her.

"Turn around. Hands on the pole, omega," I demand. She instantly follows my direction. Fuck, she's such a good girl. And she's fucking mine.

Bri's palms flatten on the rough concrete and her back curves so her ass is pushed into my groin. My fingers dip into her waistband and slide through the trimmed thatch of hair until I reach her slick pussy. "Mmmm, you're fucking dripping for me, baby."

"Please," she huffs. "Please fuck me, Tru. I need your knot."

"You know I can't knot you back here, babygirl. But I'll take care of you." I curl my fingers around the top of her tiny black spandex shorts, dropping into a crouch as I drag them down to mid thigh. The sugary fruit scent of her slick slams into me, and her thighs glisten with her arousal. Leaning in, I can't help myself as I lick up her inner leg, pausing to scrape my teeth along my bond mark before I suck it into my mouth.

Our coworkers all know we're bonded, but my mark is in a place easily hidden. Not because we're ashamed of each other, but when your livelihood depends on tips, you learn how to play the game. Bri is hot as fuck, and men throw money at her with hearts in their eyes. You'd think seeing other men flirt with my omega would make me insanely jealous, but I know who she's going home with at the end of the night. Let those hapless men pay our bills. They'll never get to taste her sweet pussy.

Pushing up on my toes, I lick a stripe through her slick folds before standing fully and to rip my belt open. My hard cock is sensitive as I pull it out, and I hiss as I drag the head through her pussy lips, coating myself in her slick. She's panting, legs trembling in anticipation, and I can't wait any longer.

Notching my cock at her tight entrance, I sink to the hilt in one, hard stroke.

# 3

There's probably something wrong with me that seeing Truett get all alpha-y and violent turns me on. But I am who I am, and as my alpha pounds into me from behind, I'm pretty fine with this quirk of mine.

Tru grunts each time he slams into my cunt, the sound accompanied by the smack of skin on skin. We've been together long enough—in life and in work—that I knew he'd need to fuck out his adrenaline. I'd had to squeeze my thighs together after his little display of athleticism, and when Lana caught sight of me, she just smirked and came to take my place behind the bar.

It's the worst kept secret that we like to bang it out back here, but we definitely aren't the only ones. The risk of being caught and watched just makes it all the hotter.

"Fuck, Bri. You feel so fucking good. Take this cock, baby." He growls in my ear just before he wraps my pony tail around his hand and pulls my head and chest back. My back arches nearly painfully, but it shifts our positions so he's hammering my g-spot on every damn thrust.

"Tru! I'm gonna... fuck!" My pussy tightens around his shaft as I approach my orgasm. I'm so fucking close.

"Fuck, yes, Bri. Come for me." He pants harder. "Come. On. My. Cock." He punctuates each word with a thrust, and I'm helpless but to obey. Heat flushes out from my core to the tips of my fingers. Truett fucks me through it, extending my pleasure as long as possible.

A whine leaves me when Tru suddenly pulls out. He spins me around, wraps his palms around the backs of my thighs, and lifts me up. I kick off my shorts just before my legs wrap around his hips as he slams back into me. My back scrapes against the concrete column he's using for leverage, but I've always liked a bite of pain with my pleasure.

"This pussy's always ready for me, isn't it baby? Such a little fucking slut for your alpha."

Fuckkk, I love it when he talks dirty. A whine ekes out and he crashes his lips to mine to smother it before pulling back to look me in the eye. "I'd say those sounds of pleasure are all mine," he smirks, "but we both know you're a screamer. Can't keep you quiet unless you're gagged on my cock."

Tru yanks my head back then bites my shoulder hard enough to leave a bruise. His thrusts are speeding up, becoming harsher, so I know he's close. Our panting echoes in the mostly empty garage, and I'm not sure I'm gonna be able to walk back to the bar the way he's railing me right now. I absolutely love it, though. My wild alpha.

"Baby, I'm—"

A scrape sounds out to our right. Truett stops speaking abruptly and we both whip our heads toward it.

"Liam," I gasp. My regular is standing there wide eyed,

an unlit joint pinched in his fingers, frozen halfway to his lips.

# 4

Holy fuck. I have to be dreaming. I must have passed out at the bar and my horniest fantasy is playing out in my sleep. Well, maybe not my *horniest*, but still.

I'm here often enough and am friends with a lot of the staff, so they let me come back here to toke up whenever I want to. The St. Patrick's Day crowd was getting stifling, and a smoke break sounded like a grand plan.

I didn't notice the moans until I was nearly right on top of them. Truett and Brianna.

Tru has Bri pinned against the thick concrete column, her tiny spandex shorts nowhere to be seen as he ruts into her. Instinct and desire have me shuffling toward the pair, but I stop abruptly when my toe kicks a loose rock across the floor. Both heads spin my direction, and Bri lets out a little gasp. "Liam—"

"Oh fuck, baby. You just squeezed my cock so hard when you saw him." Truett purrs, never taking his eyes off of me. "I knew you had a little crush on him, but I didn't know you wanted to fuck him." His thrusts slow, but don't stop.

*A crush?* Now I know I'm in dreamland. Or I'm dead and this is heaven. Either case is just fine with me. I've wanted Brianna for years, but knew she was happily bonded so I resigned myself to pining from afar. Well, from across the bar at the very least. To hear she wants me too is shocking.

What's even more interesting, there's no aggression in Truett's eyes. No warning growl in his throat. His words seemed curious, not defensive, and he's still fucking Bri while staring at me. He doesn't seem ashamed at all. Fuck.

Bri bites her plush bottom lip, her body jerking as Truett pushes into her over and over again at a slow but steady pace. My cock is hard, there's no hiding it when she glances down at my tented crotch.

"You want him too, baby?" Truett asks her, getting her attention with a nip to her earlobe. She looks at her alpha and I immediately feel the loss of her gaze like a cold winter's wind.

Still torturing that poor lip, she nods. Tru chuckles. "Words, baby. If you don't tell me what you want, poor Liam over there is going to be stuck watching instead of participating."

*Participating?*

Before I can process that, Bri answers. "Yes, alpha. I want him, too. I want you both to fuck me. Fill me up."

Jesus fucking Christ. I'm gonna come in my pants like a fucking untried pup. Is this really happening?

Truett hums. "Mmm, well, he's pretty hot. And what my omega wants, my omega gets."

Does that mean I should go to them? Stay here? Run the fuck away? My feet are frozen to their spot on the floor. Is fuck or flight a thing?

The other alpha slows his thrusting even more, making

Bri whine. "Are you joining us or what, man? Don't keep our girl waiting."

That gets me moving. When I'm just a few steps away, my nose is flooded with the scents of boozy pears and tart berries. A fierce wave of longing and possession hit me. Tru and Bri's eyes widen at the same time, likely picking up on my toasted almond scent.

"You..." Bri trails off as Truett stops moving entirely, his length still buried in his omega. *Our omega?* Will he share? Are we pack?

"Yeah," I say, brilliant conversationalist that I am.

She reaches out for me, and I'm helpless to resist. Closing the gap between us, my senses fire like lightning as her scent gets stronger. As soon as I'm within reach, Bri grips the front of my navy button down and drags me into a kiss.

Fireworks.

Her tongue demands entry and I bend to her will, licking into her ferociously. One hand cups the back of her neck, thumb caressing her jaw, while the other finds her naked hip. Bri starts wriggling, trying to roll against Truett in a plea for more. She moans into my mouth and I glance down as he pulls out of her nearly to the tip, then pushes in deep. Truett's pace slowly picks up again while Bri and I tangle tongues.

"Touch her tits," Tru growls. Bri frantically nods her forehead against mine.

Wasting no time, I push up the hem of her shirt to expose her lacy green bra. "In the holiday spirit, are we, sweetheart?" The endearment slips effortlessly from my lips. She's too impatient to banter with me, pulling the cups of her bra down to expose her hard brown nipples. She grips a breast in each hand, squeezing and kneading. Truett grasps both her wrists in one hand and pins them above her head. “Let him do that.”

My hands snap up to caress her chest, the tan flesh heavy in my palms. I tentatively massage them, trying to mimic her movements. Releasing Bri’s wrists, Tru knocks one of my hands away to pinch her nipple. Hard. Brianna cries out in pleasure. He tweaks the taut bud and addresses me.

“She’s not made of glass. She wants it rough,” he rasps, and my eyes nearly roll back in my skull. “Are you alpha enough to give her what she needs?” he challenges.

Oh, that sneaky fucker. Appealing to my nature knowing I can’t resist a challenge from another alpha. Instead of replacing his fingers with my own, I dive in and suck the tortured tip of her breast into my mouth, laving it with my tongue before I bite down.

# 5

"Yes! Liam!" I cry, my hand diving into his hair to hold him close. I've always been drawn to him, but another scent match? The myriad smells always inundating the bar mean I've never truly scented just him before. Toasted almond, reminiscent of the sweetness of amaretto and cherries.

Truett pounds into me as Liam tortures my breasts. Never in a million years could I imagine ending up here tonight, but fuck if I'm not pumped about this outcome.

"I'm close, baby," Tru growls. "Come once more on my cock so I can fill you. Then maybe Liam will be kind enough to clean you up after."

Liam's hand sneaks between my bonded alpha and me. He finds my clit and rubs tight circles, then pinches. I fly over the edge, clenching around Truett while he holds himself deep inside me and comes on a groan. Tru pulls out sooner than I'd like, but instead of putting me down, he spins me so my back is to his chest, his hands on my thighs, holding me open facing Liam.

Slick and cum leak from my pussy, but before any of it can drop to the pavement, Liam falls to his knees and buries his face between my legs. He licks into me, lapping up Truett's cum without hesitation.

Truett chuckles lowly in my ear. "Your new alpha is just as filthy as you are, baby. Good job."

When my legs start to shake, Liam stands. Licking his lips, he spears two fingers into me and rubs my g spot. I want to squirm away because I'm sensitive, but Tru holds me in place.

"Liam. I c-can't," I stutter.

"You can, omega," he replies, thrusting his fingers harder.

"And you will if you want his cock," Tru adds conspiratorially, both turning me on and granting permission for Liam to fuck me if he wants. Gods, I hope he wants.

Shockingly, my core tightens around Liam's fingers, the sudden onslaught of pleasure ripping through me as I climax once more. His fingers slip out of me, but before he can bring them to his lips, Truett grabs his wrist and lifts it to his mouth, sucking my juices off the digits greedily. Liam's eyes darken even further with lust as he watches my bonded mate.

They can explore that possible connection later. Right now, my pussy feels awfully empty. "Liam," I whine. "Please. Fuck me. Now." I sound bratty, but he doesn't seem to mind.

He quickly undoes his jeans and pulls out his hard cock. I catch a glint of metal before he steps closer and drags the head of his shaft through my soaking wet slit, coating himself in my slick, Something cold and hard passes over my clit and I buck my hips.

"Ahhh, you like that, pretty girl?" Liam purrs as he

circles his cockhead on my clit. "Ever had a pierced cock before?" I shake my head. "No? Well get ready to have your life changed."

"Damn, baby," Truett murmurs. "I'm kinda jealous right now. I've never had one either."

"You can have a ride later, alpha." Liam winks, then aligns his cockhead with my entrance and pushes forward. He bottoms out in one quick glide, Tru's cum and my slick smoothing the way. We both moan loudly.

"Godsdamn, Bri. This pussy is fucking heaven." Liam pulls out and slams back in, then grabs my ass and pulls me from Tru's hold. He pulls me up and down his cock, setting a hard and heavy pace.

Hands slide up to my breasts. Lips graze my nape. Brandy and pears assault my senses.

Truett.

"How's that piercing feel, omega? Am I gonna have to get some metal in my dick, too, after this?" my alpha teases.

"N-not if... if we k-keep... him..." Between the pounding Liam is giving me and the way Truett is licking my neck I can barely get the words out. "Keep him ar-around. Ah! Oh my gods!" Tru snuck his fingers down to rub my back entrance while I was trying to speak. Now he's using my slick as lube so he can penetrate the tight ring of muscle with a finger.

"You want to keep him, baby?" Truett works a second finger into my ass, scissoring them. Stretching me. "Think he can handle us? We can be a lot."

Liam scoffs, the sound almost offended. "I think the scent match just proves I was made to fit with you two." He tilts me back a little, changing the angle. Holy shit. "But why don't you try me, alpha?"

"Wanna see how well we share, baby?" A third digit

breaches my back entrance, making me clench around Liam's cock and Truett's fingers. "We've done this with toys, but you've never had two cocks at the same time before."

"Fuckkk." Liam groans.

I nod frantically. Yes. Yes I want that very much. It's long been a fantasy of mine, but it never felt right bringing anyone else into our pairing. Not until now. Until Liam.

Tru hums, his fingers never faltering in their rhythm. "Do you want us both in your pussy? Or should I take this fine ass of yours?" he asks.

"Fuck!" Liam shouts and stutters to a halt. "Seriously? You're gonna make me come too fast, man."

"Thought you said you could keep up, *alpha*." The way Truett draws out the designation is teasing and full of amusement. Liam closes his eyes to get himself under control while I squirm on his cock.

"My ass," I tell Tru. "Fuck my ass. I want to be full."

Truett nods against my shoulder and removes his fingers. His blunt cockhead replaces them, pressing against my tight hole. We've done anal before—there isn't a hole on my body he hasn't fucked—but this is a whole new level. Totally different than when he uses a toy in one hole and fucks the other. More intense.

"I can feel you rubbing against my cock. Fuck," Liam grits out, clearly barely holding on as Truett bottoms out.

I'm so full I can barely breathe. "Move, please. I need you to move," I beg. They don't make me wait. We stop speaking. The only sounds we make are groans and grunts of pleasure. Wet slapping noises of bodies clashing.

A haze settles over my consciousness, almost like I'm in heat, but I'm still lucid. Instead, it's almost like a whole body and soul bliss. My omega is practically screaming at me. *This is right. This is pack.*

Not one to deny my instincts, I settle my teeth over Liam's shoulder, let my omega come to the forefront, and bite.

# 6

The new bond unfurls in my soul like a fern frond after the rain. Gentle. Tentative. Seeking. A tendril of new connection easing its way into my heart.

For a moment, I'm worried because Bri didn't get verbal consent to bite Liam. Sure, he's been pining after her for years, any idiot can see that. He also acknowledged the scent match and jumped right into a threesome. But bonding is something entirely different. Permanent.

Bri unlatches her tiny teeth from Liam's skin and some of her trepidation seeps through the bond as well. For a moment, it's as if time stops and everything around us ceases to exist. No concrete walls. No cars left overnight by their party-going owners. No green beer or rowdy crowds.

Liam's eyes go dark, and he lunges forward, sinking his teeth into Bri where her neck meets her collarbone, holding her in place as he fucks up into her even harder. Ecstasy explodes from Bri's side of the bond as she comes, slick squirting all over both me and Liam. Feeling her pleasure dripping down my sac triggers my climax, and I empty my seed deep in Bri's ass, somehow keeping the presence of mind not to knot her.

I deserve a pat on the back for that one. Or a blow job.

I pull out and Liam spins so Bri's back is once more against the concrete column. One, two, three more thrusts and his knot pops into place. He roars as he fills my omega while my cum is still dripping from her ass.

*Our* omega, now, I suppose.

I lean against the wall, watching the two of them and catching my breath while I search inside myself for any hints of jealousy or anger, finding none. Bri and I aren't the type to deny the ancient instincts that are innate in every alpha, omega, or beta. It's worked for us so far, so I trust it'll keep working now as Liam joins us.

The other alpha rotates so his back is against the rough concrete instead of our omega having to bear the brunt of that discomfort. Bri peppers kisses all over Liam's face, sipping gently from his lips.

Not one to miss out on aftercare, I stumble toward them and press myself against Bri's back. She leans against me, her head dropping to my shoulder so she can look at my face. I send all the love and reassurance I can through the bond so she knows we're all good.

I trail my hands over her skin and kiss her gently. "Good girl, Brianna," I praise her. "You did good, baby. You—" It suddenly hits me that we're a true pack now. Not just a pairing, a couple. We've always wanted a pack even if it was small, but no one felt right until now. Liam settling into the bond feels like a puzzle piece dropping into place. My voice is strained when I continue. "You made us pack, baby. A true pack."

Liam chuckles. "Can't say I had 'fucking my dream girl and biting into a pack in a garage behind McGinty's' on my

2026 bingo card." Bri barks a laugh that turns into a moan when Liam's knot loosens and he slips out of her.

The familiar sound of the push-bar being slammed into by a body echoes into the garage just before someone steps through. Snarling at the threat, I cover my omega's nearly nude body, hiding her from any prying eyes.

Huh. I didn't have that reaction when Liam came through the door. Instincts are wild, man.

My snarls lessen when I recognize the interloper. Lana takes one look at us and stops dead in her tracks. Then she eyes my omega from head-to-toe and I growl at her again.

"Don't you fuckin' growl at me you alphahole," Lana scolds. "You're not a fuckin' neanderthal and I'm not gonna steal your omega. Even if she is a smokeshow."

Bri pops her head around my body, her cheeks flushed from both our sexcapades and a bit of chagrin. "Hiiii Lanaaaa," she drawls, then gives a little finger wave to the beta bartender.

Lana raises a brow and crosses her arms. "You aren't coming back to work, I take it?" She scoffs when Bri slowly shakes her head. "Figured." She sighs and walks back to the bar, pausing at the threshold to turn toward our little trio. "Get home safe."

I swear I hear her mutter lucky bitch under her breath as she closes the door behind her. The metal slams shut, leaving us in stunned silence once more.

Brianna breaks the silence. "She's never gonna let us live that down."

The garage is suddenly filled with our laughter, but as it settles over us, it sounds like a whole lot more than humor. It sounds like the bright new beginning of our journey to destiny.

It'll be a hell of a story for the grandkids. Who knew you could get lucky and find forever behind a dive bar?

# ABOUT THE AUTHOR

Clover Holloway is the cozier side of Unfortunate Reads, writing steamy monster and omegaverse romance that will make you swoon and sweat.

A long time romance reader turned author, she just can't help but make her stories cozy. She's an ADHD agent of chaos so her book topics may vary wildly, but you can always expect an HEA. She's an avid fan of traditional millennial customs including craft breweries, monstera plants, and skinny jeans.

Get lucky at cloverholloway.com.

## ALSO BY CLOVER HOLLOWAY

*Omegaverse Holiday Quickies series*

**Unwrapping the Pack**

**Bubbles with the Pack**

**Letters from the Pack**

---

**Welcome to Bone Town**

Adventure Omegaverse co-written with Thea Masen

---

**Knot Letting Go**

Olympic Omegaverse co-written with Thea Masen

---

**Slip into Me**

A short eel-shifter, fated mates novella.

*Originally published in the Strange Love charity anthology.*

---

**Taking a Tumble**

Meet cute with a dad-bod demon pet shop owner and a curvy, confident human woman.

*Part of the Ghostlight Falls series.*

**Zero to 69**

A sentient object shifter romance co-written with Thea Masen & Kate McDarris

www.ingramcontent.com/pod-product-compliance
Lightning Source LLC
LaVergne TN
LVHW090538110826
845146LV00003B/1169

* 9 7 9 8 9 9 1 3 7 4 2 9 3 *